For Indie,
with love, Giles

For Imogen and
Brown Bear,
with love from Emma xx

Text copyright © 2014 by Giles Andreae
Illustrations copyright © 2014 by Emma Dodd
First published in Great Britain in 2014 by Orchard Books,
an imprint of Hachette Children's Books

First US Hardcover Edition, December 2015
10 9 8 7 6 5 4 3 2 1
F904-9088-1-14319

Printed in China

Library of Congress Cataloging-in-Publication Data

Andreae, Giles, 1966–
I love you, baby / Giles Andreae & Emma Dodd.—First edition.
pages cm
"First published in Great Britain in 2014 by Orchard Books,
an imprint of Hachette Children's Books."
Summary: A child shares the joy of a new baby sibling, from the messy
hair above a little forehead to the two ticklish feet below pudgy ankles.
ISBN 978-1-4847-2230-5—ISBN 1-4847-2230-2
[1. Stories in rhyme. 2. Babies—Fiction. 3. Brothers and sisters—Fiction.]
I. Dodd, Emma, 1969– illustrator. II. Title.
PZ8.3.A54865Iau 2015
[E]—dc23   2014031413

Reinforced binding
Visit www.DisneyBooks.com

I love you, baby

Giles Andreae & Emma Dodd

Disney • Hyperion

Los Angeles   New York

Guess what I've got? Hip hip hooray!

A brand-new baby to love all day!

Aren't I lucky? Yes, I know!

Why don't you come and say hello?

One fat tummy, tight like a drum.

Two little cheeks on one little bum!

Two little arms, and under the vest,

One little neck and a soft, warm chest.

Two chubby legs and two rolly thighs.

One little forehead, two round eyes.

One funny hairstyle,
oh, what a mess!
Too many hairs for
anyone to guess.

Two tiny hands and

one small chin,

Eight squashy knuckles

with dimples in.

Two strong shoulders,

two little wrists.

Two plump knees,

now, what have I missed?

One squishy waist and two soft hips,

One kissy mouth with two pink lips.

Just one belly button, small and sweet,

Two pudgy ankles, two tickly feet!

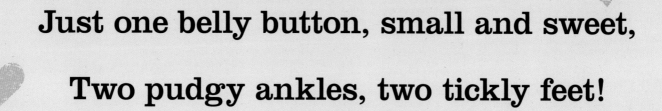

Ten little fingers, ten little toes,

Two little ears and one little nose.

Two warm cheeks, all rosy and bright,

A kiss and a cuddle to say good night.

One sleepy face on

one sweet head,

Sleep tight, love you,

it's time for bed!